EASY Samuels, B

Samuels, Barbara

Dolores on her toes

Dolores
on
Her
Toes

BARBARA SAMUELS

MELANIE KROUPA BOOKS

Farrar, Straus and Giroux ◆ New York

In memory of my father, Julius Samuels

Distributed in Canada by Douglas & McIntyre Ltd.
Color separations by Chroma Graphics PTE Ltd.
Printed and bound in the United States of America by Berryville Graphics
Designed by Jennifer Browne
First edition, 2003
1 3 5 7 9 10 8 6 4 2

Library of Congress Cataloging-in-Publication Data
Samuels, Barbara.
    Dolores on her toes / by Barbara Samuels.— 1st ed.
        p. cm.
    Summary: When her cat disappears just before Tutu Day, Dolores, with the help of her
sister, realizes that Duncan does not want to be a ballerina.
    ISBN 0-374-31818-2
    [1. Ballet dancing—Fiction.   2. Cats—Fiction.   3. Sisters—Fiction.]   I. Title.

PZ7.S1925 Do 2002
[E]—dc21
                                                                                    2001029384

"Duncan is my best friend," Dolores
would always say. "And best friends do
everything together. We read together . . .

PUSS IN BOOTS

eat together . . .

and play together.

"Whatever I'm doing . . .

Duncan helps out."

When Dolores became a ballerina,
she taught Duncan all about it.

"A ballerina must tuck in her hair . . .

and turn out her toes.
We call this first position . . .

and this an arabesque."

"I don't think Duncan likes ballet,"
said her older sister, Faye.

"Of course he does," said Dolores.
"He can't wait for Tutu Day."

On the day before Tutu Day . . .

Duncan was helping Dolores rehearse.

They were in the middle of a pas de deux when the doorbell rang.

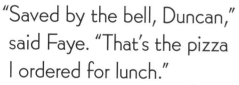

"Saved by the bell, Duncan," said Faye. "That's the pizza I ordered for lunch."

"Tomorrow is Tutu Day," said Dolores to the pizza delivery boy. "Would you care to see my arabesque?"

"Where's Duncan?" she asked at lunch. "He always eats my pepperoni."

Dolores looked everywhere.

"We'll never find him!" she cried.

"Let's check the rest of the building," said Faye. "You can borrow my Patsy Porter Junior Detective Kit."

They hurried to the basement.

"Nope," said Teddy, the building superintendent. "I haven't seen him. But I left a turkey sandwich on this table a minute ago. When I got back, there was only rye bread and a pickle."

"No," said Mrs. O'Malley, "I haven't seen him. But when I put my garbage out and turned to get my keys—crash, the bag tipped over. What a mess!"

They hurried to the front stoop.

"We haven't seen him," said Emily from the third floor.
"But we were feeding the pigeons when something
came tearing out the door."

"Birdies go bye-bye," said her little brother.

"Oh no!" cried Dolores. "Duncan left the building."

"It's time for your dress rehearsal," said Faye.

"How can I go?" said Dolores. "I have to look for Duncan."

"Patsy Porter would make signs and post them on her way," said Faye.

So Dolores made a sign.

"You made Duncan look like he just robbed a bank," said Faye.

"Good," said Dolores. "If people think he's dangerous, they'll look harder."

On her way to rehearsal, she posted copies of the sign everywhere . . .

checked the area for cat hairs . . .

and asked everyone, "Have you seen Duncan?"

When she got to rehearsal, Dolores told
the girls in the dressing room about
Duncan. They were very sympathetic.

Dolores had a hard time keeping
her mind on her barre work.

"Patsy Porter says, Try to lure the suspect back to the scene of the crime," said Faye later. So they sprinkled a trail of liver bits to their front door.

"Wow!" said Faye. "Look at all those cats!"

"But no Duncan," sighed Dolores.

That night Dolores couldn't sleep.

"Duncan is probably cold and shivering in an alley," she worried.

"His life might be hanging by a thread . . .

"What if he's been kidnapped by bandits?

"Maybe he's found another little girl that he likes more than me."

When Faye went to eat breakfast the next morning, Dolores was already up.

"Today is Tutu Day," said Faye. "What are you doing, Dolores?"

"Patsy Porter says, Try to think like the missing person if you want to find him. I'm trying to think like Duncan."

"Come have breakfast," said Faye.

TEDDY POPS

"Okay," said Dolores.

After breakfast she watched the
faucet drip. That was hard work . . .

so she took a short nap.

When she woke up, she found
a nice piece of string.

She played with it . . .

and followed it . . .

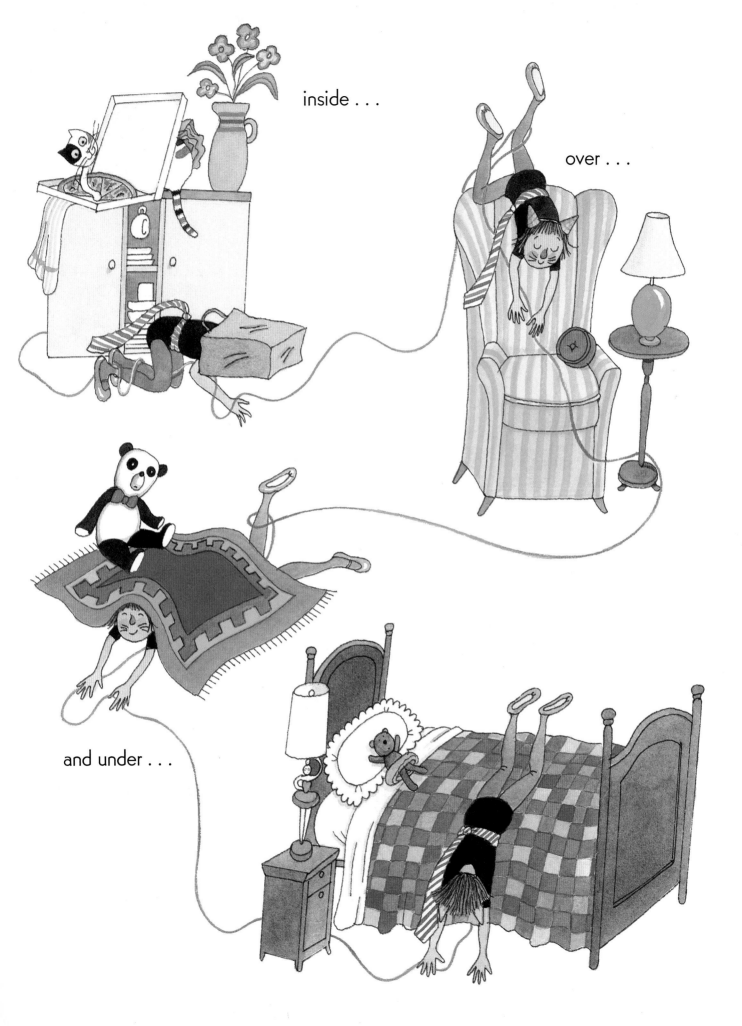

inside . . .

over . . .

and under . . .

"Congratulations!" said Faye. "You just cracked the case."

"I promise, Duncan, never to make you do another plié again," said Dolores.

"That's a relief," said Faye. "And if you leave right now, Dolores, you can still make it in time for Tutu Day."

"We'd better hurry, Duncan," said Dolores, "or we'll be late."

"You're taking DUNCAN?" said Faye.

"Don't worry," said Dolores.
"I know Duncan doesn't want
to be a ballerina. But he would
be brokenhearted if . . .

he didn't see
me dance!"

"Duncan is my best friend," Dolores says about her cat. "And best friends do *everything* together."

So when Dolores gets caught up in the world of ballet, she's certain that Duncan will want to be her partner.

But will he? When Duncan suddenly disappears, Dolores is heartbroken. Is it possible that her best friend, wearing her best tutu, has run away from home?

Leap right into another hilarious adventure with the irrepressible Dolores as she turns detective to track down Duncan—and her tutu—only to discover a few surprising things about what it means to be a friend.

BARBARA SAMUELS is the author of several adventures starring the intrepid Dolores, her older sister, Faye, and her cat, Duncan. Her most recent book, *Aloha, Dolores*, was an *American Bookseller* Pick of the Lists and a Reading Rainbow Review Book. *Booklist* praised it: "Bright and funny, the text is matched by sprightly ink-and-watercolor pictures that are crammed full of delicious detail. Almost as much fun as a trip to Hawaii."

Barbara Samuels lives in Manhattan with her husband, Nick, their son, Noah, and their Siamese cat, Guido. She did research for this book by watching Tutu Day at the Discovery Ballet Program on Manhattan's Upper West Side, where her sister Freya is an accompanist. There were no cats in the audience.